LET'S KILL SANTA

CONNOR WHITELEY

No part of this book may be reproduced in any form or by any electronic or mechanical means. Including information storage, and retrieval systems, without written permission from the author except for the use of brief quotations in a book review.

This book is NOT legal, professional, medical, financial or any type of official advice.

Any questions about the book, rights licensing, or to contact the author, please email connorwhiteley@connorwhiteley.net

Copyright © 2024 CONNOR WHITELEY

All rights reserved.

DEDICATION
Thank you to all my readers without you I couldn't do what I love.

CHAPTER 1

Considering how many years upon years I've lived in Canterbury, England and been visiting the annual Christmas markets like clockwise, I am honestly surprised I have never gotten tired of them. But I seriously couldn't, I love the Christmas markets and the ones in Canterbury are almost magical, mystical and always filled with delights.

I slowly made my way through the immense crowds of locals and tourists and university students packed tight like sardines around little brown wooden market stalls selling their delights. Everyone was dressed up in their tight black, blue and white coats as the bitter, icy wind blew down the high street.

There was a small cute family that caught my eye as I tried to glide through the wonderful crowd. The family was made up of two small toddlers being held up by their mum and dad in matching white faux fur coats as the toddlers pointed to the chocolate fountain saying that their parents should get some for them.

It was so damn cute. I loved Christmas.

The Christmas markets were filled with the sweet aromas of cinnamon, mulled wine and rich fruit cake with enough alcohol inside to knock out even the strongest troll or giant or maybe even my boss Natalia.

You see my name is Matilda Plum, a superhero in the psychology, counselling and therapy sector of the world. So I love these Christmas markets because as great as they are for my own mental health, they are the perfect opportunity to see who needs help.

The entire long, cobblestone high street was lined with small wooden stalls selling everything from weird Christmas decorations to mulled wine to sweet delightful pastries that I had already bought two bags of for myself.

I loved the sheer volume of the Christmas markets too. There was always such brilliant Christmas carols being sung (by people who could actually sing), people were laughing and chatting, and I just loved the energy that came from all of this fun.

The Christmas season was amazing to me.

I stopped for a moment and watched a smiling young woman who probably worked at the university get customers to try and guess the weight of a small teddy bear that she had. If they guessed the weight or came within a hundred grams, they won it, but I knew something was off.

As much as I wanted to continue walking about

the Christmas market trying to find a Christmas present for my two best friends Jack and Aiden, I knew I had to stop here and help out. Because something evil was going on and I had to stop it.

Thankfully my superpowers came from the myths and misconceptions that people have about psychologists, so this was just one of those powers telling me something was wrong.

There was a young boy, maybe 10, in his little black puffer jacket with his mum and dad standing behind him as he tried to guess the weight. I could sense that the boy wanted the teddy bear so badly and it would feel him with such delight.

The teddy bear wasn't anything special to me but when I grew up in the early 1900s, I never had bears or anything fun to play with so this modern world was still finding ways to thankfully surprise me.

The young woman smiled at the boy. "What do you think the weight is?"

"500 grams," the boy said so sure of himself that even I believed him.

"I'm sorry that isn't the right answer but have a sweet for trying," the young woman said.

Then I realised that the woman hadn't mentioned what the real weight was and that was what was wrong.

I went over to the young woman. "I'm sorry but what is the real weight?"

The young woman frowned. "That isn't any of your business. You might go round telling people,"

I smiled as my superpowers kicked in because she had spoken to me so I could read her mind, and just as I suspected she was cheating. There was a solid metal ball like a small marble in the teddy that made it a lot heavier than it was meant to be.

I grabbed the teddy and gently popped open the back to reveal the metal ball as it fell out and slammed onto the table.

I gave the little teddy to the boy that was beaming and as his mum and dad frowned and walked away, the little boy kept telling them how cool it was. At least I had made his day.

"I'm sorry," the young woman said.

As I was still connected to her mind I knew she was telling the truth but I didn't care anymore. She had committed a horrible crime at Christmas and she had almost ruined that little boy's day.

So I subtly implanted a little suggestion into her mind saying that whenever she wanted to cheat she would pour water all over herself. It wasn't much of a punishment and I wanted to make her pour mulled wine over herself but that would just be a waste of good wine, wouldn't it?

I went away but I turned around just in time to see the woman pouring bottles of water all over herself, and I just laughed. She clearly didn't know what the holiday spirit was all about and at least I managed to help someone today.

I was just about to continue my hunt for people to help and the perfect Christmas present for my best friends when a single phrase sliced through the air.

"Let's kill Santa,"

My superpowers cut out all other noise in the Christmas market as those words were spoken and I knew that something bad was happening.

I didn't know what was happening but I had to go and find out. Someone was in danger and I had to save them.

But if someone was willing to kill at a Christmas market then they had to be dangerous monsters.

And that scared me a lot more than I ever wanted to admit.

CHAPTER 2

Whenever me and my superhero friends start talking about the problems with being superheroes, there are always certain things that come up. Dating is a major, major issue which is always a pain in the ass because we don't age so when my partners age and we don't, things get awkward. Superpowers activating during sex is a nightmare and my personal pet hate is superpowers trying to help but not.

That was the problem I was experiencing right now.

You see I was walking through the wonderful little side streets of Canterbury that shot out like arms and legs and ribs out of the high street. They did look beautiful with their Tudor-style thick black beams leaning to one side and dirty white paint, but my superpowers weren't helping me.

I knew that I had to explore these side streets for the speaker of that voice but it wasn't clear which side street, who I was looking for and if the speaker was still there or not.

Not exactly helpful I know.

I was walking past a little coffee area with small Parisian café tables outside covered in tinsel, Christmas lights covered the street and there were a few young couples making out in shop doorways, but they weren't involved with the killing Santa plot.

I kept on walking down the side street. the aromas of sugar, mulled wine and sweet mince pies filled the air and left the perfect taste of Christmas on my tongue. And I was looking forward to the big day even more now, but then I sensed something.

The hairs on the back of my neck stood up and I couldn't help but feel like something was behind me.

I turned around and was surprised to see a fake Santa walking down the street. He was smiling and waving at the young couples and laughing with them about *not doing anything he wouldn't do at their age* and I got a really positive aura from him.

I supposed him in his little green cape and robes could have been an Agent of Santa instead of the real one, but this man had a real aura of energy about him.

"Good morning Matilda," the man said.

I had no idea how the hell this man knew who I was.

"Relax, Agent of Santa Joy Division," the man said.

I clearly wasn't as good at knowing my agents as much as I should. I knew that the Agents of Santa were the real elves from myth and legends and they were split up into three main divisions. The romance division were elves that focused on holiday romances, getting broken families back together and helping people through love.

But the Joy Division was sort of a new one for me.

"Ho. Ho. Ho," the man said waving at a little kid and he clicked his fingers and I watched Christmas magic pulse over him.

The little kid screamed in delight, laughed and his parents were filled with happiness. That was amazingly heart-warming to see.

"I can sense you aren't in the Christmas spirit little one," the man said to me.

I smiled for the sake of the other children walking up and slow the street.

"I think something is going to kill you," I said. "I heard something mention killing Santa earlier on today. I don't know who but I know it's going to happen,"

The man laughed dryly like he was already dead. "Relax little one. I am Santa and I cannot die,"

I hadn't met that many Agents of Santa before but this one had to be new and rather arrogant. No agent of Santa really tried to be the big man in front of other superheroes or agents. And I had even heard reports of Santa punishing agents that were too devoted to the image of Santa.

The man kept on talking about how silly I was being but I noticed no one else was in the side street now. There were no children about, no young couples and no parents looking for a shortcut.

We were completely alone and my superpowers told me to leave right now, but I couldn't. I had to make sure this agent of Santa was okay.

"We have to go now," I said.

"Impossible. I have presents to deliver, joy to make and children to please,"

I grabbed his wrist and pure Christmas magic burnt my hand but I wasn't letting go even if I had to teleport us away I was saving him.

Five shadowy women appeared around us.

White hot blasts struck me.

Knocking me backwards.

A woman leapt on me.

Pinning me.

The man made a candy cane appear in his hand.

He used it as a sword. He whacked the attackers across the face.

I blasted the woman with psychic energy. A brand-new superpower I found.

The woman leapt off me.

I jumped up.

Punching her.

She dodged. Punching me in the stomach.

I collapsed to the ground. I wasn't a fighter. I was a psychologist.

The woman kicked me in the stomach again. I collapsed to the ground.

The agent screamed in pain.

I looked at the agent as the woman finished stabbing him and mince pies fell out of the wounds and the agent collapsed onto the ground.

A moment later the agent's body collapsed in trays beyond trays of mince pies and the woman gave me a thumbs up and disappeared. I had no idea what was going on but even I knew that killing an Agent of Santa was a monstrous no-no.

I was even fairly sure that killing an agent was even worse than killing a God or Goddess. Whoever had just attacked and killed that agent was in for a hell of a shock because no one would rest until they were caught, punished and probably dead.

A moment later children ran down into the side street and grabbed the trays of mince pies and I had honestly had no idea whether to be disturbed or not.

They were basically eating an agent of Santa but at least they were joyous as they did it.

CHAPTER 3

There was only one thing I could possibly do as a psychologist after seeing such a horrible murder. And please, don't say or think something silly like I would do some psychological profiling because that isn't psychology, that is the biggest myth that ever existed about my great profession, and I actually have no intention of using that superpower.

It wouldn't be very useful anyway, because profiling is rubbish.

Anyway, I teleported back to my therapy office. I was a little fuming that I didn't have time to find Jack and Aiden a great Christmas present but as soon as I entered my office I loved how relaxing and soothing it was with its sterile white walls on three sides of the room and a wonderful floor-to-ceiling window that gave me a stunning view out of Canterbury. Even from here I could see the Christmas markets and everyone thankfully having fun.

There was always a good range of chairs in my

office (and it wasn't a psychological trick either. I just wanted every client to sit in their favourite chair) like bean bags, bar stools and sofas and everything in-between.

And as much as I wanted to simply sit down on a bean bag and think about what the hell I had just seen, I knew I needed to do some research hopefully my best friends in the entire world, Jack and Aiden, realised I was in here and came to ask me why I was back. Especially because after they had finished with appointments today they were meant to be meeting me down the market anyway.

I hoped their appointments were going well. For some reason we've had a lot of depression referrals lately.

I sat at my large brown desk, fired up my laptop and tried to see if there were any CCTV cameras in the side street where the murder happened. Of course I doubted the cameras would show anything because superheroes (and villains in this case) were invisible to everyone and everything when they wanted to be.

As I got a superhero friend of mine from the police sector to hook me into the CCTV system, I enjoyed the sweet orange, cinnamon and cranberry essences that filled my office. It was the purest smell of Christmas and I loved it. It might have been the best gift Jack and Aiden had ever given me.

The CCTV footage sped past me as I listened to the loud howl of icy cold wind rush past my window and I realised that the CCTV was a dead end.

Even I didn't show up on there so these attackers had to be powerful enough to also wipe me off the CCTV footage.

"Why you here?" Aiden asked.

I smiled as Aiden and Jack walked in hand-in-hand. They were the cutest couple I had ever seen and they were so suited to each other. They were both wearing a Christmas jumper each, black jeans and boots that made them look very manly and tasteful. I wished I could say the same with my black dress and leggings.

Not exactly a going-out outfit but I didn't mind.

"An agent of Santa was murdered in front of me. Five shadowy women attacked us and erased all trace of us from the CCTV footage," I said.

"Is the mince pie thing real?" Jack asked.

I laughed. "Oh yes it is. They don't bleed blood, they bled mince pies and the children love eating the pies afterwards. Their purpose is to bring joy in life, so they bring joy in death as well,"

"That's messed up," Aiden said smiling.

I could only agree. "Do you know anything about people killing agents?"

Jack shrugged and looked at Aiden. If Jack was struggling then I knew I was in trouble because both of them had spent a lot more time than me studying the history of the Gods, Superheroes and Agents of Santa.

"This isn't the first ever murder," Aiden said, "but this is the first in over a thousand years,"

"Exactly," I said. "Who would want to kill an Agent of Santa knowing what the consequences would be?"

"We have to keep this quiet though," Aiden said. "You must be aware of the Santa Crusade right?"

I nodded. I thought it was honestly a myth but every superhero worth their salt knows that after the first ever murders of agents jolly old saint Nick laughed a crusade of joy, pleasure and goodwill over all of mankind as punishment for the murders.

I know that might sound like a good thing but the world is always a careful balancing act. Good and bad must always exist in the world, so when Santa made bad impossible for a single year the world was almost destroyed.

For an entire year there were no murders, no crimes and no diseases to cure. So doctors and sheriffs and researchers (or whatever classed as those jobs back in the day) were all out of work and human progress just stopped.

When bad returned the following year no one knew what to do and that was Santa's real revenge. No one got away with killing one of his agents without punishment and whilst Santa was all about joy, love and kindness. He did have a mean streak too.

"I agree but we need help," I said. "Do we call Natalia?"

I knew that Jack and Aiden wanted to say no but we were all superheroes at the end of the day. We didn't know anything about the agents, their job and their world. We didn't know if they had enemies or creatures that hunted them at Christmas time.

We needed to know all this information and we needed to know it now.

As much as I hate to admit it I don't think these attackers are even remotely done because they said they wanted to kill Santa. And if these people could kill an agent then I have no doubt they have the balls to try killing the real thing.

The fate of the world rests on me making sure that doesn't happen.

CHAPTER 4

If you had told me when I was a little, little girl where did I think Gods and Goddesses hung out and wanted to meet mere mortals, I probably would have told you some strange story about mountains and heavens and so much other rubbish, but it turned out that the Gods hated mountains.

Most of them were scared of heights after all.

Instead me, Aiden and Jack were sitting around a little red metal table in our booth at our favourite restaurant. The walls were perfectly orange and yellow, and the rich spicy smell of tacos, tortillas and more delightful cheesy Mexican foods filled the air. I loved it here.

Of course they had wonderful Spanish Christmas songs playing in the background, the very fit male waiters in their tight black uniforms were smiling and taking our orders (we only ordered a milkshake each) and I focused on the cute young woman walking about too. She had to be a manager but she looked just as good as the men.

There weren't that many here which was a little weird because it was late afternoon and probably it was packed, but I suppose who wants Mexican food in December?

Not a lot it turns out, that just means more for little old me.

I loved Christmas time. Everyone was so happy, jolly and they weren't distracted by a crime or murder at all.

I really wish that I could have had said the same but the murder and attack and the women were just annoying me. I still couldn't believe that someone (actually an entire group of someones) had had the balls to kill an Agent of Santa.

A few moments later the most beautiful woman in the entire world materialised next to me, her long golden hair that floated in the air glowed softly and as always I was delighted by Natalia's stunning golden dress.

She was so beautiful.

"An agent of Santa's dead," I said.

Natalia frowned and she didn't speak at all. I was scared that she hated me for telling her what happened but I knew what her rageful face looked like from watching other poor unfortunate souls, thankfully this sad face was different. But she was still upset.

"Here you go," a cute male waiter said as he gave me, Jack and Aiden a massive vanilla milkshake each and Natalia magicked up her own peppermint one with a candy cane on top.

Since it was Christmas I probably should have ordered a Christmassy one, but that just showed how distracted I was by the murder.

"Tell me what happened exactly," she said.

So I did and Natalia only looked more and more furious as I went on. Jack and Aiden were as silent as the agent of Santa that was killed and even I could feel the tension in the air. Something was about to happen and I felt like Natalia was going to reveal something major.

"There have been six Agents of Santa murdered in the past two days," Natalia said. "Our sector hasn't been brought in yet because you know how they are. The Agents want to keep this done internally,"

"But they have to let us Gods and Goddesses get involved now, right?" Jack asked just a second before I could.

Natalia shook her head. "The Agents of Santa are completely divorced from us lot. They don't have their own Gods, Goddesses and superheroes and they only activate around Christmas time,"

"Why would someone want to kill them? That's what I can't understand," I said.

"Could they be wanting to kill Santa?" Aiden asked.

I shook my head. "Not likely because everyone knows whether you kill all the agents under his command or not, Santa is powerful,"

"To a point," Natalia said.

I instantly wrapped my hands around my milkshake, allowing the almost burning coldness to absorb my shock and horror.

"What does that mean?" Aiden asked.

"It means Santa isn't as powerful as he used to be now that Joey is starting to Come of Age. If Santa is killed before Joey takes over as Santa then Christmas will be erased from history,"

The words slammed into me like bullets.

"What?" Jack asked.

Natalia nodded. "If Santa dies then all the magical energy stored up in him over all the centuries, all the good deeds and all the good will that humanity expresses at this time of year will explode out of him. Imagine it like an hourglass shattering and all the sand zooming out of him,"

I couldn't imagine anything worse. I wasn't always the brightest when it came to weird workings of magic and superheroes and the Gods, but I knew exactly what would happen.

"It would be like an atomic bomb," I said, "but instead of destroying the world it would destroy Christmas and the very concept it got its power from in the first place,"

"I became a superhero on Christmas," Jack said.

I just looked at him. "That means if Christmas never happened then you never would have been made a superhero,"

"And I never would have found you," Aiden said

hugging the man he loved.

"And we never would have become friends," I said.

I finally realised just how critical this case was. Not only for the whole of humanity but also for saving the friends I loved more than anything in the world.

I had to solve this murder or at least find someone that could help me. I was a psychologist, not a detective and I didn't know the first thing about solving a crime.

Thankfully there was a very very minor division of the Agents of Santa which I was hoping could help me out.

I had to see a very old friend and I wasn't sure if they would even let me in the front door without pouring boiling mulled wine all over me.

CHAPTER 5

I first met Novilla a few years ago at a very, very hazy Christmas party I was attending for the local psychologists, therapists and other mental health professionals. I was very drunk by the time I saw her beauty, I started talking to her at the bar and one thing led to another and before I knew it it was the next day and she was in my bed. I could hardly argue with the result but I don't normally meet other superheroes that way.

Much less Agents of Santa.

I had teleported me, Jack and Aiden just outside Novilla's massive red and green wooden front door outside her small cottage on the outskirts of Canterbury. It was already pitch black now and I couldn't see anything of the surrounding areas except for the bright Christmas lights of Canterbury high street in the distance.

Novilla's cottage was stunning with its pure white walls, little windows with candles inside and the entire cottage was decorated in the most delightful Christmas lights I've ever had the pleasure of seeing. They were all sparkling like diamonds in all their reds, greens and golds. It was beautiful.

Even the air smelt of Christmas with figgy pudding, mulled wine and oranges filling my senses and making the taste of Christmas cake form on my tongue. I was so looking forward to the big day.

As much as I didn't want to knock on the door because Novilla had proposed to me once when she was drunk and I had firmly said no. She wasn't mad nor happy, she was just angry at me and Christmas.

That was why she was demoted from Romance Division to Inquisition. It was her job to investigate crimes against Christmas and other religious holidays that Santa looked after on behalf of other faiths. I honestly couldn't imagine a worse job, being forced to investigate the very worst of humanity during such a traditionally happy time of year.

But to save Jack and Christmas I had to knock.

I pounded on the door.

A moment later, the door slowly opened and the overwhelming smell of mulled wine and cheap whiskey filled my senses. I coughed on the choking alcohol fumes and I couldn't understand. Had I teleported us to the wrong house?

"Matty darling!" Novilla shouted.

Me, Jack and Aiden went inside and I was disgusted by what I saw. There were no new Christmas decorations, there were cigars everywhere, rats ran up and down the tinsel and dead Christmas trees, and even worse the Christmas wreaths were bleached white by the sunlight.

There was no Christmas joy in this house.

Novilla led us into the so-called living room where piles upon piles of Christmas wrapping paper mounted up, and little evil creatures ran around inside them. All whilst Novilla sat on her chair drinking more and more whiskey, not even brandy.

I was disgusted by what she had become.

"We need your help," I said.

Novilla shrugged. "I have drinking to do,"

"There have been six murders of your fellow Agents," Jack said. "Aren't you investigating?"

I wanted to find us a seat or something but I couldn't. Everywhere was covered in awful piles of mouldy wrapping paper. I had no idea what had happened to this once beautiful woman but she had seriously fallen from grace.

Since she had spoken to me I activated my superpowers and instantly started to read her mind and I was horrified. She hated Christmas, hated Santa, hated everything she represented. Granted she had had to investigate some truly horrible crimes over the years that happened on Christmas day but there was no need for her to do this.

Santa himself loved all of his agents, he supported them no matter what and if she wanted to change and get professional help, she could have. Santa would have helped her immediately but she didn't want help. She never wanted to change, she loved her drinking life and that was just awful.

"I investigated the killings alright," Novilla said, "I'm looking for clues at the bottom of this drink,"

She laughed and I kept searching her mind. It was clear that Novilla herself was going to be useless but that didn't mean she didn't know anything. Her new domain might have been drinking but the mind was my domain and I was now the master of her mind.

I coursed through her mind, searching for any mention of murderers or shadowy women like the people that attacked me.

Anything.

But there was a single mention. A single thought that was repeated so often that I knew it was the good part of Novilla that wanted to help me trying to tell me something important.

A few years ago Santa lost over a hundred members of the Joy and Romance Division because their leader Krampus himself had decided to rebel against Santa and punish all the nasty children and adults. But Krampus did all that and even his own supporters defected to form their own new organisation.

The Anti-Christmas Brigade, a group of superheroes focused on making sure that Christmas and all the evil things that happened during the holiday was wiped from existence.

Santa was scared of them and even though him

and Krampus were now best buddies and played golf together on the weekend. They were both scared of this new organisation.

And an organisation now had no problems killing so close to Christmas.

The very worst type of crime in my opinion, but thankfully Novilla managed to learn the address of their leader before she slipped away into a hangover and I was kicked out of her mind.

If anyone knew anything about these murders it had to be the leader of this most evil organisation.

I just hoped me and my friends wouldn't become victims 7, 8 and 9.

CHAPTER 6

"Why would I kill Santa?"

Thankfully it was hardly difficult for me, Jack and Aiden to track down the leader of the Brigade to a very expensive, posh and outrageously exclusive hotel in the heart of London. Then it was even more surprising when the leader herself allowed us entry and she had sent us mulled wine and cookies and milk.

That was an entrance I wasn't expecting.

Me and Jack sat on two very comfortable black fabric chairs in an office made entirely out of glass. I could see the floors below me and I wasn't a fan of that whatsoever. I could only imagine the floor cracking and shattering under me at any moment, that wouldn't be fun in the slightest.

The wide windows on the side that made up the walls were nice, expensive and I have to admit London was seriously beautiful at night. I was rather impressed that the office had built-in lights that fit seamlessly into the glass ceiling and floor.

I focused on the insanely beautiful woman in front of me in her angelic white dress that swept perfectly behind her as she sat down on her white desk chair. She grinned at me, but I knew she was a demon.

She was Lussi from the Icelandic folklore about a murderous demon that punished naughty children in Iceland and the adults had to protect the house and their children by marking the house with a cross.

"You always wanted to kill Santa," Aiden said standing behind us.

I tried to search Lussi's mind but she just grinned at me, my superpowers had to be the strongest out of the three of us but I couldn't break her mental shield.

"You formed an organisation to get rid of Christmas," I said. "That means you want to kill Santa and are attacking Agents of Santa to do so,"

Lussi nodded like that was a good point. I didn't like the woman very much, she might have looked good but she acted like she was in charge, was full of herself and like nothing bad could ever happen to her.

"Why would I kill Santa?" Lussi asked.

At first I didn't understand her question at all but then I realised that she was literally asking the question. Of course I doubted a powerful woman like her would actually do the killing, so if I wanted information I fully believed I was going to have to change my question.

"Why would someone from your organisation

kill these Agents?" I asked.

Lussi shrugged. "Who knows? Who cares?"

Jack leant forward. "We care. These are innocent people being murdered by your organisation?"

Lussi laughed. "Innocent you say? Do you realise how many crimes, murders and muggings are committed at Christmas time? These crimes increase because of Christmas, if there was no Christmas then these crimes wouldn't happen,"

I shook my head. "We both know the goodwill, happiness and delight that comes from Christmas significantly outweighs any bad that comes from it,"

Lussi grinned. "And anyway if Christmas never existed then I wouldn't either. So why would I want Santa dead?"

Jack stood up. "We aren't saying you killed anyone? I'm saying-"

I waved him silent and I looked around, there were no other people in this building, on this floor or anything close to Lussi and her office. If she was truly the leader of a grand organisation that was powerful enough to kill Santa then surely there would be people swarming this office building.

"You aren't a leader of anything are you?" I asked pushing my truth-telling superpower into her mind. Surprisingly enough the power took hold.

"Of course. I am Lussi I don't need anyone to help me travel to Iceland each year and punish all the naughty little children. I allow Santa, the agents and your lot to think I am all-powerful so they leave me alone. All I want is to travel, relax and explore the world 11 months of the year and then go to Iceland for the last month,"

"Why are you still here then?" Jack asked. I couldn't disagree.

Lussi clicked her fingers and her form become ghostly and I realised she wasn't even here the damn woman. She was already in Iceland and using some kind of superpower to make us believe she was here.

"Goodbye my dears and happy Christmas," Lussi said before disappearing.

I just shook my head because this was an absolute nightmare, we needed a lead, a suspect, a something to help us discover who was behind these attacks and we had nothing to show for our efforts.

We needed to go back to the drawing board, act like real detectives and find the truth no matter what.

The hairs on the bad of my neck pricked up and I instantly felt my stomach twist into a painful knot. Something very bad was about to happen.

"Ten Agents of Santa were just assassinated," Natalia said.

I instantly gasped as these attackers weren't pulling punches anymore. And that meant I had to stop too.

I had to save Jack after all.

CHAPTER 7

My heart leapt to my throat as Aiden teleported me and Jack and himself into the centre of Rochester high street, just 30 30-minute drive north of Canterbury. I normally loved the cold block-paved high street with its green, red and black Victorian shops that looked straight out of a Dickens novel.

But today I was just too shocked for words as I watched streams upon streams of children laugh, sing and dance about with little mince pies in their little hands. They were making the most of the trays upon trays of mince pies that had materialised upon the death of the Agents.

Because of how superpowers worked no human remembered the mince pies ever not being there, but it was still so weird to see so much joy and happiness and delight when I knew so much death had happened.

Up and down Rochester High Street were small wooden Christmas stalls selling all sorts of delightful decorations, gift ideas and wonderful presents from the continent. I didn't understand what had happened to these agents but they were all dead and now in death they were spreading joy.

"Where they Joy Division?" I asked knowing that Natalia had to be here.

A moment later, my beautiful boss appeared but her normal golden dress and long blond hair weren't glowing quite as bright as before and I felt sad to see her being so badly affected by this.

"Yes, all of them were Joy Division and I cannot keep this from the other Gods and Goddesses and Santa himself for much longer,"

"Too late for that," Jack said loudly over the playing of Christmas carols that filled the street.

I looked down the high street and shook my head as Joey Claus himself marched down the high street and freezing time as he went. He was a skinny little man that would only grow his fat and muscle when his father transferred power to him.

His long sweeping brown cape and trench coat pounded into him as an invisible and soundless wind tried to make him seem more terrifying than he already was.

I was surprised he was flanked by forty women in very short green uniforms, each armed with a very large candy cane twice the height of them. I didn't know if it looked comedic or weird or scary.

Probably all three of them.

"You didn't tell me Natalia, why?" Joey asked.

"Has my father not been good enough to the Gods of late? Remember you where all meant to be on the Naughty List last year but he removed you. He could always take back that special adult toy he got you,"

Natalia blushed and shook her head. "I did not tell you about the deaths because I did not want to worry him,"

"Worry him?" Joey asked smiling. "He is Santa and he feels the loss of each Agent like the death of a Reindeer and believe me, me and mum are so glad a reindeer hasn't died in over three hundred years,"

I didn't even want to ask but I simply stepped forward and waved my hand at him.

"Matilda Plum. On the naughty list three decades in a row but ended up back on the Good List in the 80s and hasn't dropped back down since," he said.

I was impressed but I honestly hadn't noticed. I guess the Naughty List doesn't mean too much.

"But if you keep thinking like that you might get added back on," Joey said.

Maybe the Lists were more important than I thought, but I did have a job to do and I was more interested in saving my friend than some dumb list anyway.

"Who's behind the killings?" I asked.

Joey frowned. "We've already investigated Krampus and his lot, you're looked into Lius and we're investigated every single other option. No one hates Christmas enough to murder an Agent of Santa, let alone over 15 of them,"

I wanted to protest and say that there had to be something else that we had all missed but my superpowers had connected to his mind and I knew he was telling the truth and he wasn't holding anything back.

He was still freezing time, a trick I could do just as easily, when I noticed there was a small group of children that caught my attention. They were covered in dirt, their little cute t-shirts were way too small for them and the way they were holding the mince pies suggested they hadn't eaten for pleasure for ages, maybe months.

And everyone knew the rumour in the superhero world. If you kill an Agent of Santa then enough mince pies turn up to feed the five thousand.

Killing 15 agents certainly allowed you to feed a ton of people.

"Natalia," I said, "where were the other killings?"

She smiled and the wonderful woman must have been reading my mind. "Chatham, Bromley in London and outskirts of Manchester and Liverpool,"

"All chronically poor areas that are deprived as hell and no one is doing anything to help them. Most kids in those areas barely have enough to eat normally let alone at Christmas," I said.

"Are you thinking something is killing Agents to provide food for the poor?" Joey asked.

I nodded. "It makes perfect sense. Rochester and Strood over the bridge is fantastically poor, Canterbury isn't too great and all the other areas are poor too. Each death means mince pies and look at who's picking up the food,"

I watched as Natalia, Jack and Aiden laughed as they realised what was going on and Joey smiled a minute later.

"The children are the only people picking up the mince pies and looking at them. They're happy, smiling and they're enjoying life for the first time in ages,"

"What do we do then?" Jack asked.

I shrugged. "I don't think we're looking for cold blooded killers here. I think we're looking for superheroes that are going to the extreme to provide for starving communities,"

"Agreed," Natalia said. "Only question is how do we stop these killers and help the communities at the same time?"

That was an excellent question and one that I didn't have an answer to at all.

But I knew if we were going to stop the killings then I had to find an answer before anyone else died.

CONNOR WHITELEY

CHAPTER 8

I never ever expected to have the son of Santa Claus sitting on a bright pink beanbag in my therapist office, but as me, Natalia and Jack and Aiden joined Joey Claus on our own beanbags, I had to admit that I was shocked.

The situation was way beyond awful and puzzling and I was so conflicted about what to do. I was so concerned that I had actually opened my peppermint and brandy-scented air fresher that I was saving for Christmas, but it did give off the most sensationally delightful smell I had ever smelt before.

The problem was rather simple in a way. We had a group of unknown superheroes from an unknown sector of the world killing agents of Santa for the sake of feeding children of extremely poor areas.

The problem if we didn't stop the killing, the lives of the Agents of Santa would be saved but the neighbours would lose out on a "good" food source. Yet if the killings continued then the Agents' lives would be saved at the cost of starving neighbourhoods.

That wasn't exactly a problem I wanted to solve but that was how dire the situation was.

"What Sector could be behind it?" Joey asked. "Me and father know nothing about your superhero world and I have sent away my escort to protect Him just in case,"

I seriously doubted that these superheroes would dare kill Santa directly but attacking his superheroes was a great way to attack him indirectly. They might as well have been killing Santa.

"What about the charity sector?" Jack asked. "I worked with them a few years ago, great people but some of them can be a bit extreme in their devotion to their duty,"

Aiden laughed. "Did one of them threaten to burn down the business districts of London as punishment for accumulating wealth that could have destroyed all poverty?"

Jack nodded. I wasn't exactly surprised but I couldn't believe that the charity folks would ever have the appetite or inclination to actually kill someone, even if it did mean helping people.

"What about the Poverty sector?" Natalia asked.

As much as I loved hearing her sexy voice I wasn't convinced. As far as I was concerned the Poverty sector was such a weird bunch of superheroes because their duties seemed to conflict with each other badly.

Half of the time they were focused on trying to get people out of poverty, but then the other half of the time they were focused on keeping people in poverty and suffering and never achieving things in life. That was evil but it was all legal according to Natalia.

"No," I said and everyone nodded in agreement.

"What about the Food sector?" Aiden asked. "What if there was some massive mince pie shortage that the superheroes were preparing for?"

"That's silly," I said grinning. "If there was a mince pie shortage across the world then a Code 2 Red Alert would be issued and we would have to raid entire countries to secure the mince pie ingredients,"

As soon as I said the words I knew how stupid it sounded, but in superhero law Code 2 was a real thing. It was just under Code 1 which was all about preventing a global shortage of birthday cake.

Something I completely agree with.

"What if all these sectors are involved?" I asked. "Think about it, we know that there are extremists in the Charity Sector, we know there are oddballs in the Poverty Sector and we know there are weirdly obsessed food scientists in the Food Sector. I bet those superheroes would love to understand how mince pies can come out of humans,"

"*Elves* thank you very much," Joey said firmly.

I didn't even bother nodding my apology. "What

do you think?"

Aiden and Jack looked at each other and frowned. I had known them for decades I knew they would agree with me shortly, they just liked to pretend I didn't have good ideas.

"What if there was a fourth sector involved?" Jack and Aiden asked at the same time.

"Sure," I said.

Natalia frowned. "The Celebration Sector,"

As Jack and Aiden started nodding I really understood that there was truly a sector for every single thing in the world of Gods, Goddesses and superheroes. Even everything to do with celebrating things, hell there was probably a god for wee at the end of the day.

I just hoped never to meet him.

"If these four sectors are involved," I said, "how do we find them?"

Natalia, Jack and Aiden shrugged because we were all psychologists at the end of the day. And that's when I realised that was exactly what we needed.

"All elves and Agents of Santa are connected right?" I asked Joey.

He nodded. "Of course I can see, hear and feel all the Agents of Santa when I wish to connect to them,"

That was good news because I wanted him to connect to the dead. "And because like human souls, elf souls don't depart from Earth for over twelve hours after death I think you can connect with the souls,"

Natalia stood up. "Excellent idea Matilda. We can see exactly what the Agents saw before they died and more importantly if they saw any faces,"

We all stood up except Joey.

"It would be risky," I said, "and we would need the power of all four of us to make it work but we can breach Joey's mind if he allows us,"

Joey shook his head. "I cannot allow that. I am the son of Santa, my mind contains top secret knowledge about the sleigh, the reindeer and Mrs Claus. I cannot give over that information for no reason,"

I focused my influencing superpower on him and added my trusting power for good measure.

"Relax," I said. "You can trust us and I promise you, we will not look at or for your secret information. I can show you how to create a mental door to lock away that information,"

Joey looked at me like he was sizing me up. "Fine,"

I grinned because we were finally going to make progress but before I breached his mind I did need to send a little psychic message to a detective friend of mine.

I wanted a detective on the case because the time of playing nicely was over. I wanted to find out who these killers were immediately.

And we were about to get one massive step

closer.

CHAPTER 9

The real reason why this was all an absolute nightmare was because there were so many thousands upon thousands of superheroes in all the other sectors besides the psychology sector that it was impossible to track down a superhero unless you knew exactly who you were looking for.

That was why we had to double check what the Agents saw before they were murdered and their corpses turned into little mince pies.

Me, Jack and Aiden all held hands with Natalia in a small circle around Joey as he stood perfectly still in the middle with his eyes shut. We had moved a whole bunch of chairs and beanbags against the wall of my office and I was looking forward to this.

I had never been in the mind of someone who worked with Santa himself before. This was really exciting. I loved being a superhero.

Me and the others all extended our minds and channelled our superpowers into Joey's mind but he locked us out.

I sensed Natalia gripping our powers tightly and combining them with hers but it was useless.

It was an immense hammer pounding against diamond. His mind was never going to open up to us.

We had failed to get inside.

"Let us in," Natalia said softly like how a lover would speak to their partner.

"I am," Joey said almost silently.

I was surprised at how relaxed he was and when I scanned his brain activity I wondered if he was dead or something. Yet his mental defences were so strong then I doubted we could breach his mind even if he was as dead as a doornail.

Jack and Aiden let go of my hands and then I realised we were making a massive mistake. We weren't dealing with a human, we were dealing with the son of Santa himself and this wasn't just any son. This was a son that was going to become Santa in a few years.

We needed Christmas magic.

"Jack go into the storage room and bring out all the spare tinsel please," I said. "Aiden go into your office and get all the Christmas food you hide there,"

He laughed and I knew he wasn't impressed that I knew about his top-secret stash.

"And Natalia," I said trying hard not to focus on her beauty, "I need you to sing some Christmas music,"

"Brilliant woman," Joey said almost silently as he

floated up into the air and turned so it looked like he was sleeping on an invisible bed.

A moment later my best friends in the entire world reappeared and I knew we had to work quickly.

I helped Jack wrap bright blue tinsel around Joey's body and then Natalia started singing wonderful Christmas songs as we set to work. Aiden placed the Christmas food (even I didn't know he had bought an entire supermarket's worth) around Joey in a circle on the floor.

Then me and Jack placed red and green tinsel all around the circle too.

The four of us grabbed each other's hands and started singing wonderful Christmas songs. We all reached out with our mind-reading superpowers and touched the surface of Joey's mind.

There wasn't a door this time to block us out but there was still some kind of defence in place. It looked and felt like a large sheet of freezing cold water that would shock a person if they were silly enough to touch it.

I implanted suggestions in my best friends' minds that they needed to focus on how Santa was real, amazing and wonderful. I did the same and I knew Natalia was sensing the thoughts from us so she did the same.

A moment later the temperature dropped and we all stood in some icy wasteland in the middle of a blizzard.

There was a sharp bite in the air but I didn't

shiver as much as I imagined I would normally. We were clearly inside his mind now and whilst I would love to explore what an icy wasteland meant to him and his mind, we didn't have the time.

I couldn't see any trees, signs of life or anything and I didn't doubt there was a reason for it. So I didn't want to be here any longer than needed.

"Show us the attackers," I said.

Jack and Aiden started singing Christmas songs loudly so they were basically shouting into the air. I didn't understand why they were doing it until I noticed something bestial lurking in the snow.

Probably another layer of his mental defences. And something I didn't want to fight.

I doubted I could.

"Show us the attackers,"

Natalia started shouting Christmas songs into the air.

Then I realised that Joey's mind was showing us the attackers. They weren't women like I believed, they had to be shapeshifting beasts or whatever.

But why were they inside his mind?

"Something's wrong," Natalia said with authority. "We were followed in here,"

I looked up at the sky. "Joey shut your mind down,"

Beasts roared through the mindscape.

Something charged.

I leapt to one side.

Something rushed past me.

I searched for a mind to connect with.

I grabbed onto something.

Images. Pain. Death. All filled my mind.

I collapsed to my knees holding my head as I screamed out in agony. It was so overwhelming and awful.

Claws gripped my leg.

I was being dragged.

Away from my friends.

Jack shouted out my name.

I shouted out a Christmas song.

The beast screamed and released me.

The wind roared around me.

Ice covered my face.

Ice covered my eyes.

My world went black.

CHAPTER 10

I gasped as my eyes slammed open and I took long deep breaths of the peppermint-scented air as I returned to my surroundings and reality. I had no idea what had happened, it had been ages since I was forced out of a person's mind because I had effectively died.

My entire body ached like a Christmas tree had fallen on me. I didn't dare move for a little while until my body relaxed and realised nothing had actually happened and it was all in my head.

That was a nightmare.

"You alright?" Joey asked as all four of them stood over me.

"She was killed inside your head. What do you think?" Jack asked.

"Those beasts were defeated," Natalia said the anger clear in her voice. "I think we were being tracked by someone, one of the other Gods no doubt,"

I wanted to shake my head but even the thought of it made my head spin at a million miles an hour.

"What were they?" Aiden asked. "They were the Trackers of Old?"

Natalia nodded. "Exactly those were once superheroes specialising in tracking game, missing people and the movement of escaped prisoners. Yet that was a long, long time ago because Christmas Eve two thousand years ago they rebelled,"

"They found a crystal containing dark magic right?" Jack asked but I didn't doubt him for a second. "The superheroes become corrupted and now they track whoever they're hired to track,"

"Who controls them?" I asked.

"Whoever summons them into this world," Natalia said. "They have the powers of all sectors to less extents. That's why they could follow us into the mind of Joey,"

"Damn," Joey said. "I don't remember,"

I forced myself to stand up and thankfully Jack and Aiden took me by the arms. I would have fallen over without them.

"What don't you remember?" I asked.

"Something about a meeting," Joey said. "I think there was a meeting about something somewhere that I was meant to do something at,"

"They stole your memory," I said. "Or at least they stole a thought of yours. It was clever using us to get information stored inside your mind,"

Joey stomped his foot. "Damn you Matilda

Plum. I trusted you and now Santa will be weakened,"

I clicked my fingers. "They didn't remove the connecting thoughts,"

"Of course," Natalia said.

I nodded. "In the human mind we create something called memory traces that are basically memories connected together and they help us to remember things. Basic cognitive psychology,

Joey shrugged. "And that helps us how?"

"We need to remember everything so far in that memory trace and we can probably understand what's missing by the other things in a trace," I said.

"Like if I remembered a cute boy, feeling in love and wanting to go out for dinner," Aiden said. "That would probably be a trace of me going out on a date with Jack,"

"Are we?" Jack asked grinning.

"Maybe later babe,"

I loved them two. So all four of us focused back on Joey and channelled our superpowers into him. We needed him to remember whatever the beasts had taken from him.

His eyes widened as our superpowers entered him and seemed to boost his memory.

"I felt happy about it," he said, "and I was excited about seeing other Agents and there was something about me seeing a Clover,"

"Who's she?" I asked.

"Clover," Joey said straining to remember. "She's an elf that focuses on speech and helping others,"

"Were you giving a speech?" I asked.

He laughed. "Never I hate speeches"

"Not the question," Natalia said.

Joey nodded. "Actually I remember feeling sad, anxious and angry at Santa for making me do it. Oh Candy canes!"

We all disconnected as we realised he had remembered what the beasts had stolen from him. And I knew it seriously wasn't good in the slightest.

"Santa's going to retire after this year's Santa run. I'm going to be Coronated Christmas Eve night just before he goes but there are traditions to follow,"

I stepped closer to him. I could see the fear, the hate and the outrage in his eyes. He didn't want to be Santa just yet.

"On the 23rd of December I have to go to the Meeting of Divisions. I have had to swear an oath of loyalty to all three Agent Divisions and every single Agent will be there to witness the oath,"

I shook my head. "Are you seriously telling me that every agent on the planet will be in one place tonight?"

He nodded.

"Where is the speech?" I asked.

"I… I don't know,"

I laughed at the dire situation I was in. Within hours all the agents on the entire planet were going to be in one location and a group of killers were after them and we didn't even know how to contact them and warn them and protect them.

And I knew Joey didn't remember either.

We only had a few hours to save a lot of lives and that meant we had to think fast.

And even I doubted we could think fast enough to save everyone.

CHAPTER 11

Over the next six hours we seriously struggled to make any progress whatsoever, and I was really waiting for a detective superhero friend of mine to actually show up, so to say I was stressed was a massive understatement.

We were all standing around in the small kitchen area inside my therapy practice with its smooth white walls, yellow splashback (definitely not my own design choice) and a black marble worktop with some kettles and mugs on it.

I loved the kitchen and it smelt heavenly of cinnamon, ginger and so many other delightful Christmas aromas, but they still weren't helping me to relax. Not one bit.

Joey was towering over all of us and he just kept shaking his head and his cloak and his cape flapped around in a wind that wasn't there and Jack and Aiden and Natalia were frowning. They wanted answers and we had run out of all possibilities.

Then I had an idea.

"The murder sites," I said grinning.

"What about them?" Joey asked the despair clear as day.

"All the murders have happened in very, very poor areas of England so far and remember the entire point of these killings is to provide food for the poor," I said.

Jack stepped forward. "That would mean we were looking for a poor area of England that hasn't been exposed to a murder yet,"

"That would be thousands of possibilities," Natalia said, "because England might be classed as a rich country when there are so many poor areas of it way below the poverty line,"

I had to agree but I was glad that Aiden was taking out his phone and searching. "But we can narrow it down further,"

"How?" Joey asked.

I went over to the marble worktop and grabbed my piping hot mug of coffee. "Remember this meeting has to fit every single Agent of Santa. How many are there?"

"Over ten thousand," Joey said.

"Right that means we can discount these ones," Aiden said focusing on his phone. "These areas would be classed as too dangerous for their anti-Christmas attacks. That still leaves us with over five hundred poor areas,"

I hated that there were so many poor areas in

England and even more people in poverty.

"Us Agents cannot be anywhere without Holly trees," Joey said.

I looked at Aiden. "We're looking for an area that is poor, has a lot of space to fit ten thousand people in and has enough Holly to sustain that many people in existence,"

"What happens without the holly?" Natalia asked.

"We die," Joey said. "That's why we always carry a small piece of Holly with us and we keep it alive with our magic. The Holly heals us, gives us life and it protects us from the corruption of doubting Santa,"

I thinly smiled. What Holly actually was was a relic or artefact that allowed Santa to use his magic to influence his elves and control them and manipulate them into doing his bidding. Thankfully, he just never ever abused that power.

"That leaves one place," Aiden said.

We all looked at him.

"Chatham is the only place that fits all that criteria," Aiden said.

"Especially with the local council creating a Holly garden," Jack said.

I bit my lip. Chatham was one of the scariest, most deadly places in all of England. There were drug dealers on every street corner, there were murders every week and punch-ups like no tomorrow. Chatham might have had the Christmas spirit but no one sensible went to Chatham of all places.

Chatham was only for the brave.

And even I doubted I had the bravery to go into Chatham without an armed escort. Thankfully I knew just the son of Santa that had his own private military escort.

"Sorry I'm late," a female voice said behind me.

I turned around and grinned as my old best friend Caroline Edwards called in wearing a jolly elf outfit, red tinsel around her neck and her sexy fit body was always a delight to see.

I hugged her and I couldn't understand why she smelt of explosives.

"I was caught up stopping a terrorist attack in Paris so I couldn't get here sooner," Caroline said.

I quickly sent everything we had on the case so far into her mind and she grinned.

"I have information that might help you then," Caroline said, "as you know I am a superhero in the Policing, Security and Terrorism sector of the world and we've been tracking five superheroes for the past year,"

Natalia stepped forward. "And you didn't think to notify us?"

"You are the Goddess of Psychology Natalia do not forget that. Your domain is the mind and not external matters. That is my domain,"

I took a small sip of boiling hot coffee. I couldn't believe that Caroline had the balls to challenge one of the most powerful Goddesses in all of creation like that.

"Of course," Natalia said holding her head high. "I was just curious. What are the sectors?"

"Food, Poverty and Charity," Caroline said, "and we have information that they're traveling to the hellhole known as Chatham tonight for a top-secret meeting. They're bringing Trackers and they're armed,"

I hated how this was going. I was going to make a decision for all of us. Rightly I should have transferred the mission and operation over to the Police and Security Sector but I couldn't allow that.

I had witnessed and started this investigation so I had to see it through.

To hell with the consequences.

"Let's go," I said grabbing everyone by the hand and we teleported away.

I just hoped we weren't too late to stop a mass murder.

CHAPTER 12

As me, Jack and Aiden stood around Joey who was flanked by his forty female elves with their peppermint candy cane staffs, I was so glad that everyone thought we were simply part of the Christmas display.

We were walking up a very long cobblestone high street with plenty of closed shops around us that looked like they hadn't been opened for decades.

The entire street was covered in little red, green and golden Christmas lights. There were even some wonderfully real plastic Christmas trees that looked so ideal and it was almost magic.

Considering the area, the entire high street looked amazing and like it was all part of some winter wonderland.

"Natalia and Caroline," I said hoping they would report into me.

"Nothing," Natalia said into my mind. "We don't even see any Santas dressed up anywhere. This isn't right and I don't like it,"

As we all walked I closed my eyes and tried to connect with the psychic mind chatter of everyone in Chatham. It was a great myth about psychologists that they could apparently sense out people's darkest fears so I had modified the myth to create a much more helpful superpower.

I searched the surface thoughts of everyone in Chatham. A lot of people were concerned about how they would afford food on the big day, other people were excited about getting presents and other people were looking forward to the drinking part.

I loved Christmas no matter the reason.

My search stopped shortly because not a single person in Chatham had any evil thoughts inside of them and whilst they probably had evil thoughts deep in their minds. I didn't have the time to search everyone like that especially without them talking to be first.

"We have to find them," I said.

Then I noticed that Joey wasn't moving and we had all noticed in the middle of the high street. There were no people there, no kids singing and screaming Christmas songs and even the Christmas lights were flickering.

On and off. On and off. On and off.

I didn't want to know what was about to happen so I looked at Jack and Aiden. "As soon as something happens we teleport Joey away,"

They both nodded and I hated not being able to

fight or do anything physically useful but at least this would give me the chance to tap into the minds of the attackers again.

Five shadowy women appeared.

Five beasts joined them.

They charged.

I didn't waste any time.

I thrusted out my hand. Looking for a mind to connect to.

I found one. I gripped her mind as tight as I could.

The attacker screamed in agony and I felt Jack and Aiden grab me.

They wanted to leave. I couldn't leave without the attacker.

I ordered her to come with us. She refused. She was in agony.

"Get him away," I said to my best friends.

They nodded.

I charged towards the attackers.

I leapt over elves.

I leapt over candy canes.

The attacker got up.

She charged at me.

My focus on her had slipped.

She leapt into the air.

Kicking me in the head.

She pinned me down.

She whipped out a dagger.

Sher raised it.

A blast of golden magical energy screamed towards us.

Smashing into the attacker.

She flew off.

The attackers screamed to each other in a language I didn't know.

The attackers teleported away.

But I connected with my attacker's mind again and I slammed my influencing superpower into her.

She couldn't move and she couldn't teleport away. She was weakened and now I could finally get some answers because something wasn't right about any of this.

But as I looked around I saw I was standing in the centre of a crate made of mince pies. So many Agents had died and in the distance I heard the cheerful, jolly shrieks of delight as children and parents came down the high street to get some free food.

Free food that had come at what cost?

CHAPTER 13

"Get away from me psych witch!"

Now I will fully admit that originally I was really tempted to simply hand over any little prisoner to the Policing Sector so their experts could perform a little interrogation for us but we didn't have time.

And I rather liked the idea of getting to know our little guest and I was looking forward to working with Caroline even more.

I had sent Jack and Aiden and Natalia to protect Joey in Jack's office so me and Caroline could be alone in my own one. I had moved all the beanbags, stools and other chairs against the walls, and I had covered up my massive, stunning floor-to-ceiling windows.

We didn't tie up the attacker but Caroline was focusing on her and it was critical that her line of sight of the prisoner wasn't broken so Caroline had to be using a superpower to hold her in place.

I was going to let her take the lead here.

"Get her away from me," the attacker said.

She was definitely something different compared to what I had been expecting. She was smaller, weaker and prettier than I had imagined.

I rather liked her little mousey face, her long raven hair and her eyes were a wonderful shade of blue. I wanted her to confess to me what she had done but I knew I had to earn her trust first.

Not exactly an easy job.

"Why do you want Matilda gone attacker?" Caroline asked. "Does she scary you? Does she make you want to repent for your crimes against humanity?"

The attacker laughed. "I am no fool I can sense the Witch trying to connect with my mind,"

She wasn't exactly wrong but that wasn't part the problem. Last time I had connected so easily with her that I couldn't understand why I was struggling to connect with her now.

I would much rather be shopping for Aiden's and Jack's Christmas present but that was life and I would make her talk to me and reveal her crimes.

"What if I came closer to you?" I asked taking two steps towards her.

The attacker screamed in fear.

That was weird and I realised that she was truly fearful of me. I don't know why but I had heard everyone knew that the Psychology Sector was the most powerful of all sectors.

Maybe I needed to use that power to my

advantage.

"Answer her questions or I will get closer," I said. I hated being so cold and harsh but lives were at stake.

"Who are you?" Caroline asked.

She didn't answer so I took a step closer. I was only three steps away from her now.

"Fine," the attacker said. "My name is Layla Fits, superhero in the Food sector,"

"And what is your purpose with these attacks?"

Layla smiled. "To kill Santa, create a food source for the poor communities of the world and cure world hunger,"

Caroline laughed but I didn't. I knelt down in front of Layla so I was eye level with her and nodded. It wasn't actually as crazy as it sounded because killing all the Agents of Santa and Santa himself would actually create so many mince pies that could feed the world.

"I understand," I said, "and it's amazing that you want to do all of this,"

Layla smiled. "Nice try psycho Witch,"

Caroline wanted to say something but I waved her silent.

"Why do you call me Psycho Witch?" I asked. "It isn't very nice and it, hurts my feelings,"

It was a complete lie and I didn't care but I wanted to see what type of person Layla really was deep down.

Layla frowned. "I'm sorry. I know you're

probably a very nice person at heart but I have to do this mission. I have to save lives,"

"By killing others," Caroline said.

I sent a warning suggestion into Caroline's mind and she frowned at me. I was making progress with Layla and I didn't want Caroline destroying it.

"Do you think this is the best way?" I asked without a hint of judgement in my tone.

"What other way is there?" Layla asked like she actually wanted an answer.

"I'm not sure but I know that killing is never the answer. What about you working with the superheroes and Gods in the Political Sector or the Charity sector?"

"I already am working with the Charity sector but they are... they're very extreme in their goodwill at times. I'm not sure they even like me,"

"But I like you. You're great," I said.

Layla grinned like a little schoolgirl at me. "You like me?"

I nodded hard. "Of course. You're clearly a good person, you want to do great stuff and I can see you only want to help people,"

"I do. I do," Layla said.

"So is killing innocent people the way to bring about change?" I asked using my trusting superpower.

"Oh," Layla said as her eyes grew wider and wider. "No. No. No. Of course it isn't,"

I understood her and Caroline smiled at me.

"I'm so sorry. I never wanted to kill anyone, oh

no how do I repent?"

I smiled at her. "I need you to open up your mind to me and give me the location of your friends and where this Agents of Santa meeting is happening,"

Layla bit her lip.

"Or I will arrest you for so many counts of murder the Gods will have to strip you of your powers and because you are so old you will die instantly," Caroline said.

I didn't correct or even challenge her. I needed this information.

Layla slowly nodded and I instantly connected with her mind. I was impressed with the mental structures inside her, there were layers upon layers of psychic defences and psychic death traps.

And it all looked perfectly natural so she clearly had a strong mind. Yet as she opened her mind to me I found exactly what I was looking for.

"London," I said. "The meeting is happening in central London. Not a poor area but it is next to tons of them,"

"Good I'll take her into custody and then I'll join you. When does the meeting happen?" Caroline asked.

"Right now," I said rushing out the door to grab my best friends and boss as we raced against time to stop a blood or mince pie bath.

CHAPTER 14

As me and the others materialised on the large stone steps of the National Gallery in Trafalgar Square I was amazed. There were thousands upon thousands of large Santas in all different shades of blues, greens and reds jumping up and down trying to keep warm in the biting wind that howled around them.

The immense screens showing Christmas adverts and special offs all around the square were shining bright, the immensely tall four columns and lions and foundation in the middle all stood strong.

There was no sign of danger yet.

Something wasn't right so I searched the surface thoughts of everyone here and they were excited, happy and filled with so much love for the holiday season.

We had to find something and quick.

"There he is!" someone shouted.

The entire crowd fell silent and the intoxicating

aroma of peppermint and Holly filled my senses as all the Agents of Santa focused on Joey who was growing larger and larger by the moment.

I could sense how much he hated this moment, hated that he would be Santa tomorrow and his relaxing life would be well and truly over.

I grabbed Jack, Aiden, Caroline and Natalia and took them over to one corner as Joey went to the middle of the stone steps waving at his fans.

"Something's wrong. Why haven't the enemy attacked yet?" I asked.

"There is too many for four people to attack," Jack said.

"Four women and five tracker beasts," I said. "That is a lot of power but the plan probably had to change after we captured Layla,"

"Did you see anything about the plan?" Natalia asked.

I looked up at the sky for a moment. I knew I had mainly focused on finding the location but sometimes my superpowers grabbed other things as well or I might have still been connected to Layla even weakly.

I didn't have anything.

"Damn it," I said.

All four of us looked out over the square and I noticed how cold the wind was. It was icy, bitter and I could have sworn icicles were starting to form on my eyelashes.

It was that cold.

"The temperature," I said, "but if the plan did change and the enemy are now trying to weaken the Agents by freezing them,"

"Does anyone thing Joey looks a little weird from the back?" Caroline asked.

I couldn't agree more as I noticed that black tendrils of energy were rising up from the back of his cloak and cape and the candy cane in his hand was turning to ash.

The very symbol of his right to the Santa throne.

"That is why I will never become Santa and that is why Christmas must stop," Joey said.

All four of us just stared at Joey as he made the declaration.

He was involved.

"I can't believe this," Jack said.

"I can," I said. "Joey is a child forced into a life he doesn't want to live,"

"And now that I have bought the four superheroes that can stop me here so they can die my goal will happen," Joey said.

"I am no superhero!" Natalia shouted.

She thrusted out her arms.

Golden magical energy shot out.

An immense black shadowy bear formed.

The energy slammed into the bear.

He deflected it.

The energy slammed into Natalia. Knocking her out instantly.

Joey seemed surprised. "Superheroes wanting to

kill Santa. An alliance of convenience is needed,"

A black cloud of black magic appeared over the huge fountain in the middle of the square and four shadowy women appeared on top.

"And so you shall have your alliance," someone said.

"Let's Kill Santa!" the other three women shouted.

The Agents of Santa whipped out their peppermint candy canes and attacked.

I rushed over to Natalia.

Her golden light was dim and she wasn't responding to my touch. Her skin was so soft, smooth and beautiful.

She wasn't going to help us here.

Caroline whipped out a gun.

She fired.

Bullets screamed through the air.

Joey slammed his candy cane into the ground. It transferred into a scythe and he sliced the bullets.

He roared at her.

Throwing her backwards.

Caroline smashed into the wall.

Jack and Aiden rushed over to me.

We gripped each other's hands.

We channelled our superpowers into Joey's mind.

He kicked us out.

He screamed slaughtered Christmas songs into our minds.

He collapsed to the ground.

I held my head.

Joey kicked me in the stomach but I just looked at him as his eyes burnt away revealing two empty sockets with fire inside, his cape became mouldy and corrupted and I realised exactly what had happened.

"You played with black magic too much," I said.

"Who are you talking to little human?" Joey said in a voice that wasn't his own.

"Where is Joey?" I asked.

The creature inside Joey's body laughed. "Dead. That young fool was an idiot. All he wanted was power and his father to die so he allowed me to consume his mind, body and soul,"

"You had no right to do that. I protect humanity's mind and you have made an enemy of me," I said firmly.

Joey gripped my head. I screamed in agony as he sent murderous thought after thought into my mind.

"You Matilda Plum are nothing. Listen to their screams as you watch them die!"

CHAPTER 15

I had no idea what this idiot inside Joey's body believed but by hell was I was sitting back idly whilst he murdered thousands of innocent people and their bodies exploded into mince pies.

I looked at Jack and Aiden. They were weak but alive and alive was all I needed to win this battle. I just had no idea how I was going to do that yet.

The idiot creature gripped my head as tight as he could. He poured all sorts of foul thoughts and screams into my mind but I was Matilda Plum superhero of the Psychology sector by hell was the mind my domain.

And my alone.

I shot every single mental superpower into his mind and he staggered back.

I stood up and I stood firm.

"You are not winning this today," I said.

The creature laughed as he hunched over like a thousand-year-old man. "You are nothing Matilda

Plum a weak little woman that has no place in the world of men,"

"These women you work with," I said, "they are smart and you know they will never let you escape,"

The creature grinned. "And I will reveal my true form to them when they have created the mince pies I will corrupt and make sure only adults eat them,"

I was shocked. That was evilly clever and just flat out wrong.

If that was true then he would and could turn millions of English adults into his mindless servants that would kill, corrupt and could take over the world for him.

I had to stop him but only Natalia could kill the demon outright.

"Natalia corruptus!" the creature shouted.

Black magical energy crackled around Natalia.

I rushed over to her.

A force of energy whacked me away.

I charged forward.

Natalia's golden light turned black.

She stirred. She sweated. She fought.

I blasted psychic energy at the creature but it did nothing.

I blasted every single mental superpower I had at Natalia.

She deflected it but it wasn't Natalia. Not the woman I secretly loved more than anything.

Her hair was falling out and her long golden dress was torn and corrupted and her eyes were deranged.

Natalia shot out her arms.

Smashing me, Jack and Aiden against the wall of the national gallery harder and harder. The screams of the Agents of Santa got louder and louder.

They were dying. I was dying.

Natalia walked over to me, Jack and Aiden as we all struggled to stay alive as I felt my bones compressed together and my brain expand.

My vision blurred by I knew my Natalia was in there and she wouldn't kill us.

I blasted a mental command into her mind and her focus shifted for just a moment. But a moment was all I needed.

I threw my weight to one side and gripped Aiden and Jack's hand just as Natalia started to press up into the wall again.

We all combined our superpowers and we smashed our way into Natalia's mind.

The creature was new here and Natalia's mind was kicking up a hell of a firestorm to stop the demon getting to her critical systems.

I had no idea what her mind looked like. There were fires everywhere, hurricanes of death and destruction ripped through it all and it was a single swirling, whirling mess.

I relied on instinct to show us the way. I trusted Natalia to lead us to where we were needed.

Then I saw a little blood red creature running around in the corridors of her memories and mind.

The three of us shot out our hands and the creature froze.

"Get out," I said.

The creature smiled. "You have no power here Matilda Plum, you are a weak woman,"

"Get out!" Jack and Aiden shouted as I watched a large tendril of fire shoot up the back of us.

The creature laughed. "You two are just weak gays pretending to be men. None of you have power over us demons,"

Aiden gripped mine and Jack's hand and we all smiled.

"A lot of people have told us that," I said and Natalia's entire mind vibrated with magical energy.

"Get out!" we all shouted into Natalia's mind.

Her mind screamed and roared and sang in utter happiness as bright white light exploded through her mind cleansing all of the demon's taint and corruption.

I released Jack's and Aiden's hand and we entered reality to finish this once and for all.

CHAPTER 16

As soon as I opened my eyes and fell off the wall of the National Gallery, Natalia flicked her eyes and healed us instantly. I was so damn happy that Jack and Aiden were okay and the love of my life was okay too.

All four of us went over to Caroline and she was still unconscious but I saw out of the corner of my eye Joey starting to escape.

We all spun around and Natalia flicked her wrist and the demon froze. We went over to the creature as he snarled, screamed and wanted so badly to rip us limp from limp but it was over.

"I know Joey is dead," I said, "but there were other ways if Joey is still in there. You have ruined your life granted,"

"That explains Joey's growing power," Natalia said. "Santa wasn't transferring it, it was the demon getting stronger inside him,"

I was disgusted with what Joey had done and

whilst he never deserved to die, he would have made an awful, awful Santa.

Natalia went over to the demon and punched it in the head. As soon as her divine fist touched the creature it shattered into ash and even the ash glowed bright gold as it was burnt away.

And the demon was well and truly dead.

"Help!" someone shouted.

I spun around as the four evil women and their five beasts kept on attacking. And I realised that Layla was still a player here.

Each of the women had to have a tracker beast attached to them and their Will so there had to be some part of Layla that the beast was responding to. Otherwise the beast wouldn't keep attacking.

I instantly reconnected with Layla's mind and searched it. She was trying to keep me out now and she was watching the slaughter unfold through the beast's eyes.

I had to shut down the connection.

I felt Natalia's mental warmth along with Jack's and Aiden's love as they joined me in my psychic search.

"Watch out," I said.

I could sense Layla was making sure the creature charged towards us but Agents of Santa were jumping in the way before exploding into mince pies.

I had to find out how to stop this.

"The brain," Natalia said. "We have to shut down the brain regions,"

We all nodded as if we shut down her brain for even a little while then it would cut the connection between the beast and Layla.

I started singing *We Wish You A Merry Christmas* with the others as my very cute backing chorus. Layla's eyes flickered and I knew our singing was drowning out her wants, desires and thoughts.

She wanted to hear the Christmas music and I sensed Natalia using her sleeping superpower to make Layla fall asleep.

Within moments we disconnected just as the beast was about to strike.

I looked at the beast as it started to look a little confused like he didn't know why he was standing there and he didn't know where he was in the world.

"Your contract is fulfilled," Natalia said, her hands glowing seductive golden light.

The immense bear-looking beast nodded and then howled and all the beasts disappeared.

And the entire crowd and battle went silent as no one understood what was going on, and my eyes immediately watched the four remaining women frown at us.

Two of them were bleeding real blood and the Santas next to them were leaking small bite-sized mince pies onto the ground.

"Enough of this mince-pie-shed," I said. "You are attackers and you have committed many crimes against humanity and the laws of the Gods and Goddesses. You must answer for your crimes,"

"But what about the poor? What about the starving? What about the fact that so many get to enjoy Christmas by overeating, over drinking and overindulging but millions of innocent people don't?" one woman said.

I nodded. "We will sort that one out but just surrender,"

"Never!" one woman shouted as she blasted an Agent of Santa into mince pies.

She was about to blast another one but Natalia clicked her fingers and time stopped around that woman. Freezing her in a gap between seconds.

"Surrender," I said walking down the steps of the National Gallery, "and I promise you we will do something about the poor this Christmas and we will do something to help them next year too,"

The three remaining women didn't seem sure and whilst I couldn't see their faces shrouded in shadow I could sense they were weighing up their options.

"Fine," the women said as one. "Arrest us but know these changes nothing. Christmas is awful, the poor are struggling and the poor will never be helped by anyone else,"

As Caroline awoke and arrested the four women, I just shook my head. This was all so much mince-pie-shed that could have been avoided.

But I was more than going to try to keep my promise, we had to do something to help the poor, I just had no idea what.

CHAPTER 17

Normally on the day of Christmas Eve, I love to spend time with my friends, travel about helping people and making sure that every single person has the best possible Christmas they can, and this year I did actually do that, and then some.

For the past day, me, Jack and Aiden have been running around and jumping from poor area to poor area all over the world, let alone the UK, secretly gifting poor communities and the starving the secrets to bettering themselves and giving them enough food to last them into the new year.

We secretly told some poor single mothers some ways to improve their lives, make their money go further and how to break the cycle of poverty their families had been in for generations. I really hoped we managed to help them and we did that for more people than I ever care to admit. We helped some people who were ready to hear what we were secretly implanting in their minds but others simply forgot it.

We made plenty of children laugh, screaming with delight and giggling as we went street to street, area to area, and as the icy cold wind blew past us I really had to admit I loved it.

But now with the dim sun setting and night veiling the sky, and me, Jack and Aiden sitting exhausted on our massive black sofas around a magical roaring fire, I couldn't believe how tired I was but also how pleased I was. Of course we couldn't help everyone on the planet but I liked to believe we helped more than enough people to make good on our promise.

The bright red, orange and blue light from the dancing flames flickering on the white walls of the living room and made the ancient pictures of my family almost come alive on this most magic of nights.

Because soon we would go to bed and wonderfully wake up to lots of wonderful presents under the tree, I was still annoyed with myself that I hadn't managed to get Jack and Aiden any presents yet but I was a superhero, I was sure I could teleport into a store tomorrow morning, leave some money on the counter and get something before they even noticed.

That was the current plan anyway.

Jack and Aiden cuddled up together on the sofa, they were so cute, sweet and warming that I realised I truly loved them. They had never been my friends, they were always my family, my loved ones and the only people even I would kill for.

And I was so glad that this mission had worked out okay because it meant that Santa and his Agents were okay, so Christmas was still in existence and Jack had still become a superhero. I would hate to imagine how awful my life would be without him in it.

I honestly would have hated my life.

"We have a confession," Jack said gesturing I should come over on their sofa and join in the hugging.

We had all slept together after drunken nights out so I had no problem hugging them, so I went over to Jack and hugged them tight.

"We didn't get you a present," Aiden said. "You do so much for us. We don't know how to repay you,"

I laughed and it took me a few moments to realise that I wasn't laughing because I had done the same thing, but because it was silly.

"You two just being here with me, being my family and being yourselves is my gift. It sounds silly and corny but it's the truth," I said.

Jack and Aiden's eyes went watery and so did mine. I seriously loved these guys.

I was about to get out my phone and play some Christmas songs when we heard four massive pounds on the roof and the fire went cold as someone slid down the chimney. I hadn't cleaned the thing for ages.

"Show off," Natalia said as she appeared next to

me in her normally beautiful golden dress that illuminated the entire living room in breathtaking gold.

A few moments later a very overweight man with a clean-shaved face and wearing a long brown hiking jacket appeared in front of us covered in soot.

"Ho. Ho. Ho. Don't you ever clean that thing?" Santa asked.

"Am I on the naughty list?" I asked.

Santa smiled. "Maybe you should. Mrs Claus only bought me this jacket ten minutes ago,"

I laughed because I had no idea why I was talking to Santa of all people.

"Nick," Natalia said, "tell them why you're here,"

Santa smiled. "Ho. Ho. Ho. Thank you all for saving me and my Agents because of you now Christmas joy, romance and mystery can explode out in the world this Christmas. And I can continue,"

Natalia smiled. "And the rest Nick. I know you don't like asking for help but you need to,"

Santa's smile weakened a little but I knew it was still warm despite my mind-reading superpowers being blocked.

"Ho. Ho. Ho. Well with my Agents dying and my reindeer going on strike because I changed the brand of their food I need some help. Would you three do me the honour of driving my backup sleighs?"

"Back up?" I asked.

Natalia nodded and rolled her eyes. "His sleighs always break down on the Himalayas, Area 51 and the

Bermuda Triangle so he needs the backups available and go directly to him,"

I just grinned. I had always wanted to fly with Santa and help deliver presents so now I was actually going to.

"And I think he needs a little joy tonight after losing his son," Natalia said.

I couldn't agree more and as Santa smiled, laughed and told a few jokes to Jack and Aiden he allowed his mental defences to slip and I entered it. I could sense all the joy, excitement and desire about the mince pies he'd eat over the course of the night, but there was also sadness. Profound sadness.

I would go with Santa to make sure he was okay because he had lost his son to the worst way of them all, demon possession, not a pretty way to go in the slightest.

"That's brilliant," Jack said in response to a Santa story.

All of us including Natalia stood up, held hands and as we teleported away I was so looking forward to tonight and this was honestly the best Christmas present I could give myself or anyone else. Without me and the others Jack wouldn't be here and this amazing opportunity wouldn't be happening either.

Because I was going to travel the world tonight with Santa, and come on, who wouldn't love that and thankfully I'm able to.

I love my job, I love Christmas and I seriously love being a superhero. Happy Christmas everyone.

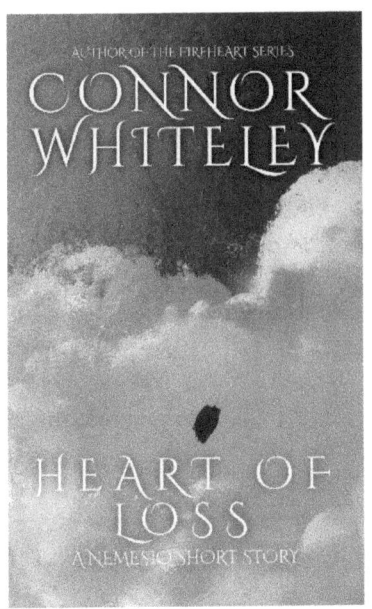

GET YOUR FREE AND EXCLUSIVE SHORT STORY NOW! LEARN ABOUT NEMESIO'S PAST! And get signed up to Connor Whiteley's newsletter to hear about new gripping books, offers and exciting projects. (You'll never be sent spam)
https://www.subscribepage.io/fireheart

About the author:

Connor Whiteley is the author of over 60 books in the sci-fi fantasy, nonfiction psychology and books for writer's genre and he is a Human Branding Speaker and Consultant.

He is a passionate warhammer 40,000 reader, psychology student and author.

Who narrates his own audiobooks and he hosts The Psychology World Podcast.

All whilst studying Psychology at the University of Kent, England.

Also, he was a former Explorer Scout where he gave a speech to the Maltese President in August 2018 and he attended Prince Charles' 70th Birthday Party at Buckingham Palace in May 2018.

Plus, he is a self-confessed coffee lover!

Other books by Connor Whiteley:

Bettie English Private Eye Series
A Very Private Woman
The Russian Case
A Very Urgent Matter
A Case Most Personal
Trains, Scots and Private Eyes
The Federation Protects
Cops, Robbers and Private Eyes
Just Ask Bettie English
An Inheritance To Die For
The Death of Graham Adams
Bearing Witness
The Twelve
The Wrong Body
The Assassination Of Bettie English
Wining And Dying
Eight Hours
Uniformed Cabal
A Case Most Christmas

Gay Romance Novellas
Breaking, Nursing, Repairing A Broken Heart
Jacob And Daniel
Fallen For A Lie
Spying And Weddings
Clean Break
Awakening Love
Meeting A Country Man
Loving Prime Minister

Snowed In Love
Never Been Kissed
Love Betrays You
Love And Hurt

Lord of War Origin Trilogy:
Not Scared Of The Dark
Madness
Burn Them All

Way Of The Odyssey
Odyssey of Rebirth
Convergence of Odysseys
Odyssey Of Hope

Lady Tano Fantasy Adventure Stories
Betrayal
Murder
Annihilation

The Fireheart Fantasy Series
Heart of Fire
Heart of Lies
Heart of Prophecy
Heart of Bones
Heart of Fate

City of Assassins (Urban Fantasy)
City of Death
City of Martyrs

City of Pleasure
City of Power

<u>Agents of The Emperor</u>
Return of The Ancient Ones
Vigilance
Angels of Fire
Kingmaker
The Eight
The Lost Generation
Hunt
Emperor's Council
Speaker of Treachery
Birth Of The Empire
Terraforma
Spaceguard

<u>The Rising Augusta Fantasy Adventure Series</u>
Rise To Power
Rising Walls
Rising Force
Rising Realm

<u>Lord Of War Trilogy (Agents of The Emperor)</u>
Not Scared Of The Dark
Madness
Burn It All Down

Miscellaneous:
Dead Names
RETURN
FREEDOM
SALVATION
Reflection of Mount Flame
The Masked One
The Great Deer
English Independence

OTHER SHORT STORIES BY CONNOR WHITELEY

Mystery Short Story Collections
Criminally Good Stories Volume 1: 20 Detective Mystery Short Stories
Criminally Good Stories Volume 2: 20 Private Investigator Short Stories
Criminally Good Stories Volume 3: 20 Crime Fiction Short Stories
Criminally Good Stories Volume 4: 20 Science Fiction and Fantasy Mystery Short Stories
Criminally Good Stories Volume 5: 20 Romantic Suspense Short Stories

Connor Whiteley Starter Collections:
Agents of The Emperor Starter Collection
Bettie English Starter Collection
Matilda Plum Starter Collection
Gay Romance Starter Collection

Way Of The Odyssey Starter Collection
Kendra Detective Fiction Starter Collection

<u>Mystery Short Stories:</u>
Protecting The Woman She Hated
Finding A Royal Friend
Our Woman In Paris
Corrupt Driving
A Prime Assassination
Jubilee Thief
Jubilee, Terror, Celebrations
Negative Jubilation
Ghostly Jubilation
Killing For Womenkind
A Snowy Death
Miracle Of Death
A Spy In Rome
The 12:30 To St Pancreas
A Country In Trouble
A Smokey Way To Go
A Spicy Way To GO
A Marketing Way To Go
A Missing Way To Go
A Showering Way To Go
Poison In The Candy Cane
Kendra Detective Mystery Collection Volume 1
Kendra Detective Mystery Collection Volume 2
Mystery Short Story Collection Volume 1
Mystery Short Story Collection Volume 2
Criminal Performance

Candy Detectives
Key To Birth In The Past

<u>Science Fiction Short Stories:</u>
Their Brave New World
Gummy Bear Detective
The Candy Detective
What Candies Fear
The Blurred Image
Shattered Legions
The First Rememberer
Life of A Rememberer
System of Wonder
Lifesaver
Remarkable Way She Died
The Interrogation of Annabella Stormic
Blade of The Emperor
Arbiter's Truth
Computation of Battle
Old One's Wrath
Puppets and Masters
Ship of Plague
Interrogation
Edge of Failure

<u>Fantasy Short Stories:</u>
City of Snow
City of Light
City of Vengeance
Dragons, Goats and Kingdom

Smog The Pathetic Dragon
Don't Go In The Shed
The Tomato Saver
The Remarkable Way She Died
Dragon Coins
Dragon Tea
Dragon Rider

<u>All books in 'An Introductory Series':</u>
Clinical Psychology and Transgender Clients
Clinical Psychology
Moral Psychology
Myths About Clinical Psychology
401 Statistics Questions For Psychology Students
Careers In Psychology
Psychology of Suicide
Dementia Psychology
Clinical Psychology Reflections Volume 4
Forensic Psychology of Terrorism And Hostage-Taking
Forensic Psychology of False Allegations
Year In Psychology
CBT For Anxiety
CBT For Depression
Applied Psychology
<u>BIOLOGICAL PSYCHOLOGY 3RD EDITION</u>
<u>COGNITIVE PSYCHOLOGY THIRD EDITION</u>
<u>SOCIAL PSYCHOLOGY- 3RD EDITION</u>
<u>ABNORMAL PSYCHOLOGY 3RD EDITION</u>
<u>PSYCHOLOGY OF RELATIONSHIPS- 3RD</u>

EDITION
DEVELOPMENTAL PSYCHOLOGY 3RD EDITION
HEALTH PSYCHOLOGY
RESEARCH IN PSYCHOLOGY
A GUIDE TO MENTAL HEALTH AND TREATMENT AROUND THE WORLD- A GLOBAL LOOK AT DEPRESSION
FORENSIC PSYCHOLOGY
THE FORENSIC PSYCHOLOGY OF THEFT, BURGLARY AND OTHER CRIMES AGAINST PROPERTY
CRIMINAL PROFILING: A FORENSIC PSYCHOLOGY GUIDE TO FBI PROFILING AND GEOGRAPHICAL AND STATISTICAL PROFILING.
CLINICAL PSYCHOLOGY
FORMULATION IN PSYCHOTHERAPY
PERSONALITY PSYCHOLOGY AND INDIVIDUAL DIFFERENCES
CLINICAL PSYCHOLOGY REFLECTIONS VOLUME 1
CLINICAL PSYCHOLOGY REFLECTIONS VOLUME 2
Clinical Psychology Reflections Volume 3
CULT PSYCHOLOGY
Police Psychology

www.ingramcontent.com/pod-product-compliance
Ingram Content Group UK Ltd.
Pitfield, Milton Keynes, MK11 3LW, UK
UKHW020049301224
452836UK00012B/365

9 781917 181938